★ American Girl®

Wellie wishers™

Sunny Day Scavenger Hunt

Scholastic Inc.

americangirl.com/service

ISBN 978-1-338-25428-0

10 9 8 7 6 5 4 3 2 1   18 19 20 21 22

Printed in the U.S.A. 40
First printing 2018

Book design by Carolyn Bull
Animation art direction by Jessica Rogers and Riley Wilkinson

Splish-splash. Splish-splash. Emerson stomps through the puddles in the garden. She sings as she goes.

"It's raining, it's pouring! The silly bunny's snoring!"

"Emerson!" her friend Ashlyn calls. "Come join us!"

Emerson runs to the tea table and joins the other WellieWishers: Camille, Willa, Ashlyn, and Kendall. But just as she sits down, the rain stops.

"Aw," Emerson says. "Now the puddles will dry up."

"That's okay," Camille says. "Rainy days that turn into sunny days are my favorite. Look—the colors in the garden are so bright!"

"Hey, that gives me an idea," Ashlyn says. "We should have a sunny day scavenger hunt to celebrate the colors! Everyone picks a color, then whoever finds the most things of their color in the garden wins."

"Sounds terrific!" says Kendall.

"You mean *color*ific," says Emerson.

The WellieWishers laugh.

"I can keep score," Camille says. She uses a pencil and paper to write down everyone's colors. "I pick blue, for the water where the mermaids live."

"I choose yellow, like my rubber chicken," says Emerson.

"Red for me, like my wheelbarrow," says Kendall.

"I pick brown, for the squirrels," says Willa. "What about you, Ashlyn?"

Ashlyn stands up tall, her chin in the air. "I choose orange, like my favorite orange marmalade. And just so you guys know, finding colors is my specialty, so I'll probably win."

The WellieWishers line up to start their scavenger hunt.

"On your mark . . ." Camille says slowly. "Get set . . . not just yet . . . almost . . ."

"Camille!" Ashlyn says eagerly.

"GO!" shouts Camille.

The WellieWishers are off! They begin searching high and low for their colors.

"Oh, I see two blue things already!" cries Camille. "My shirt and the stripe on my skirt."

Ashlyn frowns. "Those don't count. You're supposed to find colors in the garden."

"But I *am* in the garden," Camille says. She draws two lines on the scorepad for herself.

Over by the flower patch, Emerson finds a yellow daffodil. "A point for me!" she calls.

"And one for me," Willa adds. "This stick is brown."

Camille draws two lines on the scorepad for Emerson and Willa.

A couple minutes later, Kendall shouts. "Bingo-bango! I found a juicy red strawberry!" She shows it to the others, holding it tight.

Squish.

"Oops." She giggles. "Does it still count?"

"Yep," Camille says, drawing on her scorepad. "A point for Kendall."

"Everyone is doing great," Camille tells Ashlyn. "Well, almost everyone."

"That's because they picked easy colors," Ashlyn replies. "There's got to be something orange around here somewhere. I'll get a point any second. Let's keep hunting."

They look near the Garden Theater Stage. Ashlyn digs deep in the dress-up chest.

She pulls out a blue wig, a red scarf, and a yellow scarf.

That means points for Camille, Kendall, and Emerson. But not Ashlyn.

Next, they look by the big tree. Willa is there.

"I'm finding so many brown things!" she says. "The squirrels. The tree. Even the mud is brown! And it's fun to jump in, too. See?"

She takes a big leap and—

SPLAT!

"The mud is also *messy*, Willa," Ashlyn mutters.

Suddenly, Ashlyn has an idea of where she can find *lots* of orange things. "Come on, Camille!" she says.

The girls race to the vegetable garden . . .
only to find Carrot the bunny eating the last
orange carrot.

"Ugh!" Ashlyn shouts. "This is the worst!"

Just then, Kendall walks by with her wheelbarrow. It's
filled with red things.

"It's not fair!" Ashlyn says to Camille. "Everyone's finding
stuff with their color, and I can't find anything orange."

"I'm sure you'll find something soon," Camille says.

But Ashlyn pouts. "Easy for you to say. You already have
lots of points."

Ashlyn keeps hunting. But everywhere she looks, she sees yellow, red, blue, and brown.

All the WellieWishers are earning points except for her. She's going to lose the game!

"That's it! I'm done!" Ashlyn shouts. "I don't want to play anymore!"

She grabs the scorepad and rips the paper out.

"What's wrong?" Camille asks her quietly. "I thought we were having fun."

Ashlyn sighs. "The scavenger hunt was *my* idea, but I'm not finding anything orange. I told everyone I was the best. What will they think?"

"They'll think you need a little help searching," Camille says kindly. She calls the other girls over and fills them in.

"Of course we'll help you find something orange," Emerson says.

"Yeah," Kendall says. "We can go on an orange-erific scavenger hunt."

Ashlyn takes a deep breath. "Thanks, you guys. I'm sorry I ripped up the book."

"Forget about the book," says Camille.

"And forget about keeping score," adds Willa. "Let's all just have fun."

Ashlyn likes that idea.

Once again, the WellieWishers are off!

They try by the garden gate first. They don't find anything orange, but they do find some perfect mud puddles to jump in.

Next, they try the playhouse. They don't find anything orange, but they do find some puppets, so they put on a quick puppet show.

At the Garden Theater Stage, they still can't find anything orange . . . so they decide to sing a silly song about it.

Finally, they end up right back where they started.

"I can't believe we couldn't find anything orange," Willa says.

"That's okay," Ashlyn replies. "I had fun anyway!"

"Me too," the other WellieWishers say.

Suddenly, Camille points up at the sky. "Look!"

"Whoa! Talk about colorific!" Kendall says. "We finally found something orange."

"And red, and yellow, and green, and blue, and purple!" Ashlyn says. "It has all our colors!"

Before they go back to playing, the WellieWishers spend a few minutes admiring the rainbow.

They all agree it's been a wonderful day in the garden. Their sunny day scavenger hunt was a huge success. And not because anyone won—because they all had fun playing together!

Wellie wishers™